WINDMILL BOOKS

I Can Draw People

Contents

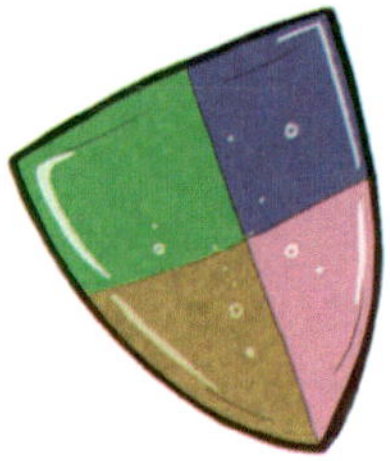

Knight

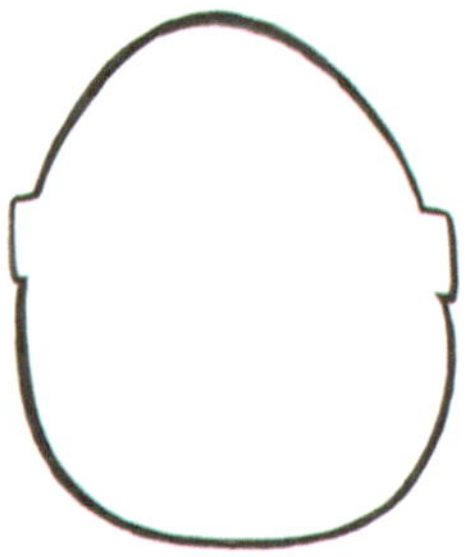

1. Draw an egg shape for the helmet.

2. Pencil in the visor, hair, and face.

3. Sketch the shield with four panels.

4. Add the knight's belted tunic.

5. Draw the knight's legs and boots.

6. Finish by drawing an arm, hand, and sword.

Queen

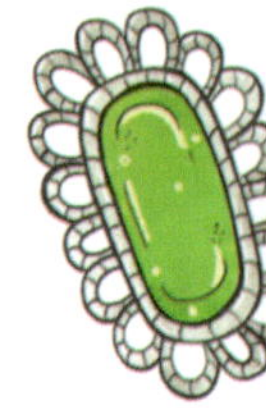

1. Draw a jeweled royal crown.

2. Leave a space and draw a face and ears.

3. Add the Queen's hair and earrings.

4. Draw a neck and upper half of a dress.

5. Add the Queen's arms and hands.

6. Draw the full skirt and more jewelry.

Superhero

1. Draw a head, ears, and hair.

2. Add details to the superhero's face.

3. Sketch a neck, T-shirt, and belt.

4. Draw legs, tights, and boots.

5. Pencil in arms for the superhero.

6. To finish, add the cape and a superhero logo!

Ballerina

1. Draw a head, ears, hair, and a face.

2. Add a bun on top and curly locks near the ears.

3. Pencil in the neck and top of the leotard.

4. Draw the ballerina's tulle tutu.

5. Add legs and ribboned slippers.

6. To finish, draw arms and a hand.

Soccer Player

1. Draw a head, ears, eyes, a nose, and a mouth.

2. Sketch in pigtails and bangs.

3. Pencil in a V-necked soccer shirt.

4. Draw arms, upper legs, and shorts.

5. Sketch in gloves, socks, and shoes.

6. To finish, draw the soccer ball!

Athlete

1. Draw the lower half of the face. Add ears.

2. Sketch in a sweatband and curly hair.

3. Pencil in the running shirt.

4. Draw the athlete's pumping arms.

5. Sketch the baggy running shorts.

6. Add legs, sneakers, socks, and action lines.

Swimmer

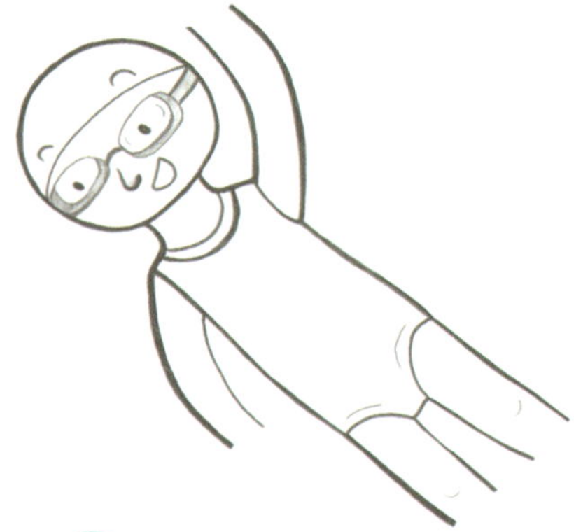

1. Draw a head, swim cap, goggles, and face features.

2. Sketch a neck and one-piece swimsuit.

3. Add arms and upper legs.

4. Draw hands, lower legs, and feet.

5. Add a pattern to the swimsuit.

6. To finish, add some water and shading.

Police Officer

1. Draw a semicircular cap with a head below.

2. Sketch in the ears, brows, eyes, nose, and mouth.

3. Add a band and badge to the cap.

4. Draw the shirt, pocket, and badge.

5. Add the belt, buckle, arms, and hands.

6. Draw pants, shoes, and a two-way radio.

POLICE

Firefighter

1. Draw the firefighter's helmet.

2. Add the head, ears, and face details.

3. Pencil the long-sleeved jacket.

4. Now, draw pants and sturdy boots.

5. Sketch hands and a fire hose and nozzle.

6. Add stripes to the jacket and some water coming from the hose.

Lifeguard

1. Draw a head, ears, hair, and face details.

2. Sketch the neck, T-shirt, and shorts.

3. Draw arms, hands, legs, and shoes.

4. Give the lifeguard a rescue float.

5. Add a beach patrol flag on its pole.

6. To finish, sketch a cross on the T-shirt.

Astronaut

1. Draw a circle with curved lines inside.

2. Sketch the details of the face.

3. Draw an oval for the body.

4. Add hair, rings to the helmet, arms, gloves, legs, and boots.

5. Add some valves and an air tube to the helmet.

6. To finish, add the control panel to the astronaut's suit.

Farmer

1. Draw a face. Add bangs and a hat.

2. Draw the ears, neckline, and chest.

3. Sketch overalls and strap buckles.

4. Add booted legs and a hand holding a basket of apples.

5. Draw an arm and a hand, a pocket, and some stitching.

6. To finish, sketch braided hair and the shirt pattern.

Vet

1. Draw the head, ears, hair, and face.

2. Add the neck, lab coat, and shirt.

3. Add pants and lace-up shoes.

4. Draw a happy pup next to the vet.

5. Pencil in the vet's hands and a leash for the dog.

6. To finish, draw the vet's glasses and stethoscope.

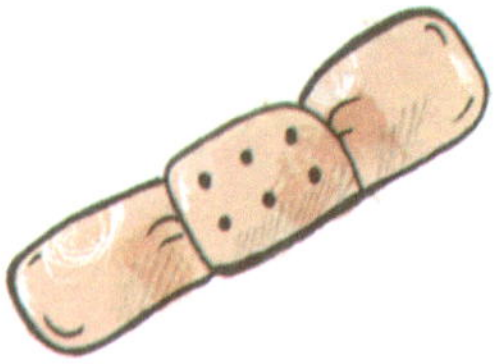

Nurse

1. Draw the lower half of the head and face.

2. Add ears, hair, and a shirt collar.

3. Draw the rest of the nurse's shirt.

4. Sketch pants and shoes.

5. Pencil the arms and hands.

6. Add a pocket watch and name badge.

Baby

1. Draw a potato shape for the head.

2. Pencil in an ear on each side of the head.

3. Add details to the face and wisps of hair to the head.

4. Draw the baby's chest, tummy, and diaper.

5. Now, add waving arms and hands.

6. To finish, draw the legs and soles of the feet.

Published in 2019 by Windmill Books,
an Imprint of Rosen Publishing
29 East 21st Street, New York, NY 10010

This edition is published by arrangement with Green Android Limited

Created and Produced by Green Android Limited
Illustrations by Grace Sandford

Cataloging-in-Publication Data

Names: Sandford, Grace.
Title: I can draw people / Grace Sandford.
Description: New York : Windmill Books, 2019. | Series: I can draw
Identifiers: ISBN 9781538390153 (pbk.) | ISBN 9781508197294 (library bound) | ISBN 9781538390160 (6 pack)
Subjects: LCSH: Human figure in art--Juvenile literature. | Drawing--Technique--Juvenile literature.
Classification: LCC NC765.S264 2019 | DDC 743.4--dc23
Manufactured in the United States of America

CPSIA Compliance Information: Batch BW19WM: For Further Information contact Rosen Publishing, New York, New York at 1-800-237-9932